Published and distributed by

 ISLAND HERITAGE
P U B L I S H I N G

94-411 KŌʻAKI STREET, WAIPAHU, HAWAIʻI 96797
ORDERS: (800) 468-2800 • INFORMATION: (808) 564-8800
FAX: (808) 564-8877 • **islandheritage.com**

ISBN# : 0-89610-792-2

First Edition, First Printing - 2003

Little Spring Eggs

A Lift-A-Flap Book

Written by Ellie Crowe • Illustrated by Yuko Green

To Andrew, Karlie, Katie, Luke, Maria and Mikayla—

With love,
Aunty Yuko

❀ ISLAND HERITAGE

One spring day in Hawai'i . . .

Down by the sea,

Where the palm trees grow,

A big blue egg went CRACK!

Inside the egg a baby bird chirped, "Oh no!

I've grown much too big for my egg.

Hey, someone, let me out—I'm ready!"

And he waited and waited.

But nothing happened.

Down by a meadow,

Where the green grasses grow,

A round white egg went CRACK!

Peck, scratch, kick, push. "I'm ready!"

Out of the egg came...

"Here's a juicy worm," hooted the mama owl.

"Nice," hooted the little one.

Meanwhile . . .

Down by the sea,

Where the trade winds blow,

In a big blue egg,

The baby bird chirped, "Hey, you guys out there!

I'm ready and I'm willing to come out of here. "

And he waited and waited.

But nothing happened.

Under the sea,

Where the pink anemones grow,

Teeny tiny orange eggs went POP!

Wiggle, wiggle, squirm, squirm. "We're ready!"

Out of the eggs came...

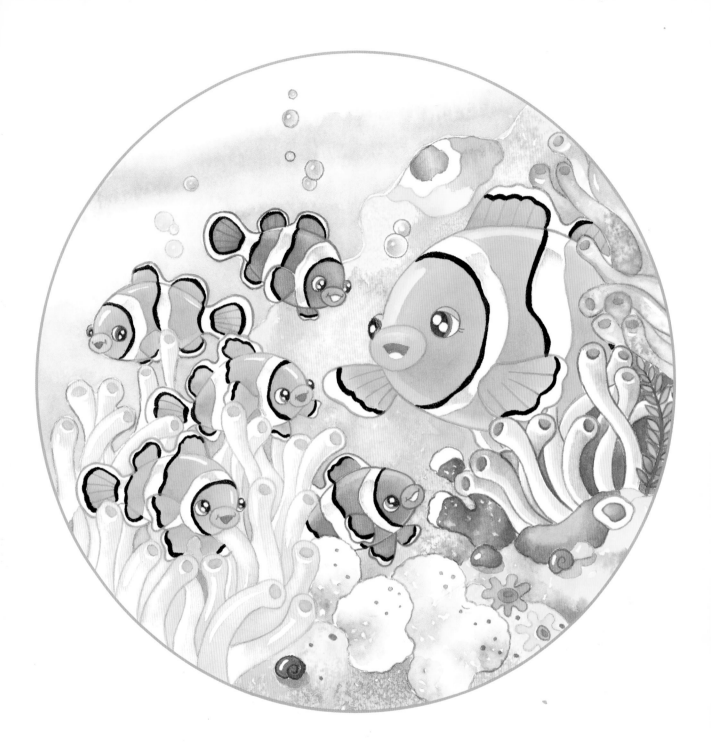

Swish swish went the mama clownfish's tail.

Swish swish went the little ones.

Up the slopes of the volcano,

Where the dark lava flows,

Three creamy white eggs went CRACK!

Peck, peck, kick, kick. "We're ready!"

Out of the eggs came...

"Here's a juicy red berry," squawked the mama nene.

"Yummy!" squawked the little ones.

And still . . .

Down by the sea,

Where the red hibiscus grow,

In a big blue egg,

The baby bird chirped,

"Let me out of this egg right now!

I'm tired of waiting for some action."

And he waited and waited.

But nothing happened.

Down by the pond,

Where the water lilies grow,

Lots of floating tiny jelly eggs went POP!

Wiggle, wiggle, squirm, squirm.

"We're ready!"

Out of the eggs came…

"Ribbit, ribbit," croaked the mama frog.

Wiggle wiggle went the little ones.

Deep in the rainforest,

Where the ʻōhiʻa trees grow,

Two white- and brown-speckled eggs went CRACK!

Squirm, scratch, peck. "We're ready!"

Out of the eggs came...

"Sip this juicy flower," squeaked the mama ʻiʻiwi.

"We will!" squeaked the little ones.

Down by the beach,

Where the naupaka flowers grow,

Six round white eggs went CRACK!

Peck, push, wave those flippers.

"We're ready!"

Out of the eggs came…

Flip flop went the flippers of the mama turtle.

Flippety flop went the flippers of the little ones.

And still meanwhile . . .

Down by the sea,

Where the blue waves flow,

In a big blue egg,

The baby bird chirped, "Turn me loose!

I'm a prisoner in here."

And he waited and waited.

But nothing happened.

Down in a garden,

Where the white plumeria grow,

A small yellow egg went CRACK!

Wiggle, wiggle, gnaw, gnaw. "I'm ready!"

Out of the egg came...

Flitter flutter went the mama butterfly.

Wiggle wiggle went the little one.

Down in a little Hawaiian home,

Where the soft lights glow,

Two small leathery eggs went ZAP!

Wiggle, wiggle, wave those tails. "We're ready!

Out of the eggs came...

"Here's a crunchy bug," chirped the mama gecko.

"Chik-chik," chirped the little ones.

Finally . . .

Down by the sea,

Where the purple liliko'i grow,

In a big blue egg,

The baby bird chirped, "If nobody's going to help me,

I'll have to help myself."

Peck, scratch, wiggle, push.

"I did it! I did it!"

Out of the egg came...

"Clever baby! Here's a munchy crab," chirped the mama booby bird.

"I like it out here!" chirped the little one.

The End!